www.facebook.com/mattshawpublications

Dead End

Written by Matt Shaw

PROLOGUE

To my right there is a glass mirror built into the wall which stretches from one side of the room to the other. I have seen enough films to know that there will be a group of people standing on the other side of it, looking through at me, yet I'm not confident enough to give them a smile.

The grey, plastic chair that I sit on rocks thanks to an uneven leg. I doubt it left the manufacturers like this and yet I can't figure out in my head what could have possibly warped it so. There is a suited man sitting to one side of me. He was assigned to me by the government as I do not have my own lawyer. He is friendly enough in his offer of assistance but not friendly enough for me to ask whether he can think of what possibly could have happened to the chair. It shall remain one of life's mysteries and - to be fair - I probably have greater things to be concerned about right now.

We are sitting at a table.

On the table is a white plastic cup of lukewarm water. On one end of the table, up against the wall, there is a tape recorder which has been loaded with a tape cassette. With technology moving ahead so fast, I am surprised to see such an antiquated device. I guess the government has more important spending to be doing elsewhere, especially when these recorders do their job so well. *If it's not broke, don't fix it.* The device is recording and capturing what the gentleman opposite is asking. Wait. What was he asking?

I looked at him blankly.

'I'm terribly sorry,' I said, 'I zoned out.'

The gentleman looked towards his suited colleague, seated next to him, and then back at me. With what can only be described as a moderate amount of patience, he asked again.

'We were hoping you could save us all a lot of time,' he said, 'and tell us what happened.'

I hesitated a moment. I have no qualms about telling him my story. I have nothing to hide. But that's not to say I deserve to be spoken of, or looked upon, as a piece of dirt. I've worked hard my entire life and my taxes pay this man's wage. I do not deserve to have him looking down his nose at me, or looking at his colleague as though I am insane.

'I'd sooner you didn't talk down to me,' I told him. My heart was racing. Usually I didn't tend to voice my opinion. The way I see it, opinions are like assholes and everyone has one. And - just like people enjoy the sound and smell of their own singing assholes, they also like to hear their own opinion. More so when they can force it upon an unwilling partner. With that in mind, I find it easier to keep my opinion to myself because it saves for arguments further down the line. Well, I say that but, I really can't stay quiet over this. I continued, 'I've had a long and - as I am sure you're only too aware - stressful day. I am tired, both mentally and physically and, to be frank, I would rather have a twenty minute nap than discuss this with you. But, for the sake of moving things along and getting this done so you can attend to more pressing matters, I am setting aside the possibility of a nap to be a good citizen. So, I would appreciate it if you treated me with some decorum and respect.' I stopped talking.

The gentleman looked at me for a moment. His face was expressionless - but not for long as he burst into what one can only describe as a fit of laughter. He turned to his - so far - silent partner and elbowed him on the arm.

'Can you believe this guy?' he asked.

His colleague said nothing. He just continued to look at me with utter contempt.

I sighed. Perhaps I needed to be clearer.

'In other words,' I continued, 'let's get this done but - in the meantime - try not to be a complete cunt about it, yes?'

The suited fellow next to me choked on his laughter as the room fell silent.

'Now,' I continued for the sake of moving things forward, 'where would you like me to start?'

There was a pause.

'Perhaps,' the gentleman said, 'we can start at the beginning?'

I nodded.

'So,' I said, 'to the beginning of the story.'

I lifted the plastic cup of lukewarm water and took a sip whilst trying my hardest to look as though I appreciated their offer of beverage.

THE TRIP (PART ONE)

1.

I was driving with my wife. We were in a camper-van which we had rented from a reasonably priced company on the Internet. The rental was for a road-trip initially planned a year previous - back when we were still on talking terms. We always booked our trips early. With our financial commitments stretched, it made it easier to save for them if we were paying them off bit by bit. It sounds stupid but if we ever thought we wanted a holiday, and that we would just save monthly, the cash would always somehow get swallowed up in some unexpected debt. At least by just booking the trips up front, even if a bill came along that we hadn't counted on, we would just have to deal with it. Yes, some months were harder than others and - sometimes - it even added extra stress on our way of living *but* we'd always know we had a vacation to look forward to. Of course, that went very wrong when - in this instance - our relationship crumbled before the start of our planned holiday.

I'll still call her my wife because - for all intents and purposes - she *is* still my wife. We have agreed to part ways. We have agreed to remain amicable for the purpose of this trip. We are not a couple though and - when the trip is over - this will be made official through the courts. I'm not sad about it and neither is she. We've both had plenty of time to come to terms with it.

Despite being on enough speaking terms to agree to enjoy "one final trip together", my wife was giving me the silent treatment. At various points in the quiet drive I'd attempted - unsuccessfully I hasten to add - a little small talk with which to break her icy walls down. The walls didn't even crack, let alone start to crumble though. The bitch was as stubborn as a spunk stain on Monica Lewinsky's dress. She was as "crusty" too.

When driving on a long stretch of road with clear views all around, I would occasionally glance in her direction. She'd be reading her book, or looking at a map, or staring out of the window thinking of whatever women think about. I, myself, would sit there idly wondering whether she thought this silent treatment was actually punishing me. Or, did she know that I enjoyed it? Three hours now, give or take, and she hadn't uttered a word other than to call me a "prick" when I nearly side-swiped a cyclist. Three hours of silent bliss.

'Are you getting hungry?' I asked.

She didn't answer me. I wasn't surprised. She's so stubborn that she could be starving half-to-death and still refuse to answer me. She'll wait for me to say that I want to stop and - then - she will moan that we're stopping.

I glanced at her. Her eyes were closed as though she was pretending to be asleep.

'Really?' I broke the silence again. 'Unbelievable.'

We drove another hundred yards or so in silence.

'We're stopping soon,' I warned her. 'I'm getting hungry, I'm getting tired. And we can work out where next on the agenda to visit.' Still my words were met with a stony-silence. With the road ahead clear of traffic, I gave her another casual glance. She was still pretending to be asleep.

Remember - I told you - this bitch is stubborn.

Still, the silent treatment? If this lasts the whole vacation, it could well end up being our best trip yet. I turned my attention back to the road. I smiled.

JUST THE BASIC FACTS

2.

No one starts a relationship with the aim of breaking up. When you first get together with someone, you imagine that person to be *the one*. You want to experience all you can with this person. You want to see the sights, you want to explore, you want to laugh, you want to love. As time goes on, you may want more than that; you may want pets to share your home, you may want children of your own. Each and every couple is different but all have the same *want*. They want happiness and - if you have ever been there - you would know that a break-up brings nothing but misery, even if you are the one who is stepping back. At the start of *any* break-up there is always pain. The pain is obvious if you're the one being left and less-so if you're the one doing the leaving. But imagine, in leaving someone, you still have to see your partner getting hurt. This person that you once had loved. Even if they have changed into someone you dislike intently, if you're human - chances are you still won't like seeing them sad. Although you could look at it from another angle; you could be happy that they're hurting. After all, you could be leaving them because they had cheated on you, or pushed you around one too many times. Why would the break-up be hard then? Because it's still a conversation you have to have which is going to bring stress. They'll be pleading for you not to leave or they'll be demanding their stuff back. Then there will be an adjustment period where you find yourself living alone again - or back with parents, or crashing on a friend's sofa - but you'll still be getting text messages from the other half, begging you to try again or just giving you shit for daring to leave them. *It is still stressful.* So, yes, no couple gets together dreaming of a future where they can split up from one another. At the start of any proper relationship the futures always centre around a life together filled with happiness and dreams.

My wife and I were no different.

We wanted a future.

We wanted to be happy.

We wanted to explore the world together, despite not having two pennies to rub together.

We even spoke of having children together. In fact, our first argument - if you can even call it that - was because she wanted a girl and I wanted a boy. At the end of the day though, whatever that child would have been, we both would have loved it unconditionally. Anyway you can't really call that a serious argument. If anything it was reminiscent of the time she'd told me she was a cat person despite knowing I was a dog person. For the record, we had neither cat nor dog. We owned a fish tank which, for the first week, remained empty of life as we struggled to get the various levels right to give them a good and happy life when we did buy them.

One of our fish got sucked up into the filter and died but that's another story.

When I met Alisha, I never set out to find someone to marry. In truth I wasn't even looking for a girlfriend at the time. I was working hard in my job and most of my time was sucked up with that, and general bullshit which

- at the time - seemed important. Looking back though, it never was - it was just an excuse to hide away from the real world and, funny thing is, I don't even know why. At that stage of my life - early twenties - I hadn't been hurt, I hadn't had my heart broken... I was just content with being "just me" I guess. Anyway some friends had dragged me out and "out" was where I met Alisha.

Alisha and I hit it off more or less straight away. I can't remember when our friends left us exactly but - at some point during the night - it had ended up just being the two of us sitting at the bar, cradling our drinks and laughing. When we realised our friends had disappeared, it didn't even cross our minds to go and look for them. We just shrugged it off and ordered another round in. By the end of that night, we'd learned so much about each other and realized how much we shared in common. We even shared what would be our first kiss. To this day I don't know if it was a happy coincidence or whether our friends had planned our connection but - I don't try and dwell on it too much. It wasn't important how we came to be. It was just nice that we'd found one another.

I had proposed to Alisha at Christmas. We had been together for six months and were already living with one another. It was her, me and a small fish tank in the corner of the living room. There was turkey cooking in the kitchen - just the crown, there was no sense in roasting a whole bird for just the two of us. Our presents were wrapped and piled neatly beneath the tree. We wouldn't open them until after our dinner but I was getting anxious as I knew one of the gifts, funnily enough the one in the biggest box, was the ring with which I wanted to ask for her hand in marriage.

'We could open one present each now,' I suggested.

She refused. It was "tradition", apparently, to wait until after dinner. Not to me though. When I was growing up we would open the presents first thing in the morning. Then, once the presents were done, my mother would disappear into the kitchen to finish making the dinner she'd already prepared. That was how I liked my Christmas mornings to go. Waiting, even without knowing what I had planned, was no fun and didn't "add to the excitement", as she put it. It was just frustrating.

Thankfully - when the time did come round - she opened the big box to find a smaller one packed inside. Inside of that, another smaller box and so on, so forth until it got to the last one. She burst into tears when she saw the ring and immediately said "yes" when I managed to pop the question. It was a good Christmas, despite the remainder of the day being spent with Alisha phoning around her friends and family members.

'Hey, guess what... He asked me to marry him!' she would say to whomever answered the call.

Less than a year later and we were married on what I could only describe as the happiest day of my life. That's kind of funny given how the marriage turned out though, right? Surely, upon looking back, I should regard the day with resentment? It was, after all, the day I ultimately set myself up for a fall for later in my life.

*

The gentleman sitting opposite me straightened his tie and cleared his throat. I'm not sure if the throat-clearing was because he was sitting there trying not to chew upon a lump or whether he was using it as a way of breaking my flow. I looked at him with a raised eyebrow and gave necessary pause for him to be able to speak should his heart so desired.

He looked at me and leaned ever so slightly closer.

'Perhaps we could skip forward to the part where your wife died?' he asked me.

I looked down at the plastic cup of water before me. During my recounting I appear to have finished the last of it. Following the officer's lead, I too cleared my throat.

'May I have another cup of water?'

'After,' he said coldly.

I glanced at the chap to my side. He paid me no attention, neither telling me to continue with my story nor to join my metaphorical side and demand a full cup of water for me. Slowly I turned back to the officers before me.

THE TRIP (PART TWO)

3.

I had been driving for most of the morning now and hadn't once stopped to relieve myself, despite needing to. With a service station fast approaching I knew it would be my last chance to use the bathroom and get something to eat for a little while so - without communicating with Alisha - I turned into the car park to find a suitable parking space. I'm sure you can understand that parking camper vans isn't as easy as parking a car. Some car parks have narrow spaces, seemingly too narrow for holiday-makers such as myself, and other car parks are just so busy there is little hope in finding anything but an empty motorcycle space which, obviously, is not good enough. Mercifully, there were plenty of spaces on this occasion and - no sooner had I pulled up in one - I turned the camper's engine off.

Thankful to stop finally, I just sat there a moment. I would be lying if I didn't say my whole body was aching from the drive. My brain hurt from the constant thinking too. It was okay for Alisha, she had completely shut down having refused to drive for me because - and I quote - "it's too big". I could make a quip about female drivers at this point but, without knowing the audience properly, I was always told to watch what you say. It is better to sit in silence and look a fool than to speak your mind and have it confirmed. I cannot recall where I'd heard that saying before but, they were words to live by.

The service station was of a good size. There was a little newsagent which - undoubtedly - sold over the price confectionary, useful for parents wishing to silence their children. There was a fast food restaurant serving up the local stray cats (I guess) and there was a pub-style cafe offering an All-Day-Breakfasts for the weary traveller. I myself fancied a fry-up, I have to admit.

'I could eat a horse,' I said.

Now I couldn't actually eat a horse. At least, not in one go. I don't even think I know a single person who could but - that's another story. It was, I believe, just a saying to convey a feeling of utter hunger. More than that though, it was something to say with which to break the silence I was still being subjected to. When no reply was given, I continued, 'I'm going for the fry-up. What do you fancy?'

I looked at Alisha. She was just staring ahead at the service station. She didn't look impressed but - on the plus side - her eyes were at least open. She looked at me with a look I had got used to in the time since our marriage first started to crumble. I remember the first time she gave me such eyes; it had actually hurt my feelings. I don't recall having done anything to warrant such a look back then, but - when we had talked about it - apparently I had been an idiot. I asked her how but, surprise surprise, she couldn't remember *that* bit. I argued that it couldn't have been that bad then which, in turn, meant I probably *hadn't* deserved the look. That, in itself, had earned me "the look". *Men are from Mars, women are from any place that's better.*

I asked again, 'Hungry at least?'

'I'm not eating there.' There was no suggestion of an alternative place to eat. No compromise. Just a flat out refusal to eat here. It was this kind of attitude which irritated me. If you don't fancy eating somewhere, or even going someplace, at least have an alternative to offer. Don't just slam the door and lock it shut. And, yes, of course, I am aware that there isn't actually a door and it hasn't actually been locked. I am - obviously - speaking metaphorically.

I looked back at the service station. There was the junk food option but I know she'd turn her nose up at that too. She never really has been into junk food. *I can't eat that, I'm watching my figure.* There had been a temptation, when she had made such a comment, to point out that the "figure" had disappeared long ago but I bit my tongue. Such a remark would merely be picking a fight for the sake of it. The last thing I want, after driving all morning, is to pick a scrap.

I pointed out, 'There's probably some sandwiches in the Newsagent?'

She looked at me coldly. There seemed to be nothing behind her eyes; no thoughts or whatever else. I choose not to question her though because - whatever *is* there, I know I won't like hearing it.

'Well I'm hungry,' I told her. 'I need to get something to eat before we carry on driving.'

'Fine,' she said.

I had been around long enough to know that "fine" is not a good word to hear from a woman.

'Well I can't very well go and eat and leave you in here,' I told her. 'Why don't you come in and...'

'I'm not coming in.'

I was going to suggest she browse the menu on the off-chance that there could be something worthy of her attention but, when she was like this, there was little point. Clearly she was itching for an argument. My fault, I guess. I did wake her up early this morning so we could hit the road before the traffic built up.

'Well I don't know what you want to do,' I said as I put my foot down, 'but I need to eat. If you want to stay here and sulk...'

'I'm not sulking!' she snapped.

I paused and laughed.

'What's so funny?' she asked. This was another dangerous question which women liked to ask.

'Nothing.'

She wanted an argument and, very nearly, I almost gave her one.

'Look, I'm hungry. I'm going to go inside and grab something to eat. I would really like it if you'd join me...'

'I'm not hungry.'

I paused a moment and then rolled my eyes. This was going to be a conversation I would never win.

'Whatever.'

I opened the driver's door and jumped down from the vehicle before slamming it shut. Without looking back I started my walk towards the building. As I did so, I couldn't help but wonder as to whether I should have turned back. I didn't want to make it up to my wife. I didn't want to apologise. She was being unreasonable. I just wondered whether I should have left the window open a little for her. I didn't want some do-gooder showing up, screaming that the bitch couldn't breathe. It was, after all, a warm day.

Best not, I thought.

As was usually the case in places like this, the breakfast was overpriced and smelt a million times better than it looked and tasted. Knowing they were the only place around to serve such food, and that they had a captive audience, the owners clearly didn't give a second thought to what they dished up on the chipped plates. It was still better than nothing though. The taste was also tarnished by the fact that I knew I was in the dog-house. Again, I am not saying I was literally in such a building. The dog-house is - once again - metaphorical. A place in which I have been cast by the hand of a cruel, unfair wife who - no doubt - was sitting in the camper van thinking that *I* was the asshole. Frustrated, I sat back in the uncomfortable chair and looked around the room. Cleaners were going from table to table merely pushing the grime around as opposed to actually cleaning it, an elderly man was sitting in the far corner (I couldn't help but to wonder whether his wife was also waiting in the car) and there were some children treating the area as a playground whilst their slob-like parents sat by, paying them little to no attention. It was hardly the most relaxing of breakfasts, I have to admit.

'How's your food?' a young waitress asked me. She'd been the one to take the order from me and - whilst she was friendly enough - it was obvious she hated this job and held a special kind of contempt for her clients. Regardless, I tried to be nice.

'Fine,' I said - using my wife's well-worn but favourite word.

The waitress was probably used to people being grumpy with her. Most people who come in have been on the road for x amount of hours. Most are tired. Most are hungry. Their moods would most likely be short and she would be an easy target.

I smiled at her.

'If you need anything…'

'Actually - do you have a box, or something?'

'A box?' She looked at me and raised a well-groomed eyebrow.

'Yeah - something I can take it away in. I'm running late and it might be better to eat on the road,' I told her. I figured this was better than saying, *I've left my wife in the camper van and I am feeling a little guilty about it, even though it's her own damned fault.*

'We can do that,' she said helpfully.

'That's great. Yes please then.'

She picked my plate up and walked back with it to the kitchens where she could box it up. As I waited, I looked back around the room. These places are such miserable places. You'd think they wouldn't be. People here are clearly passing through so you would think they were on their way somewhere nice, somewhere which would cause them to be a little more excited but - no. Everyone looks so miserable. But then, they probably think the same about me.

They'd have no such thought if they'd met my wife. If anything, they would be sympathetic.

TAKE IT FROM SOMEONE WHO KNOWS

4.

The problem with relationships - in fact, people in general - is that we often believe ourselves to be correct in what we say. I mentioned about keeping politics and thoughts to myself because, it doesn't matter what I believe, there'll always be someone there to argue with me and, when they do, I don't want to hear their opinion because, as mentioned, I will believe it to be wrong. I guarantee you're the same, even though you will - of course - deny this.

As I had been sitting in the "restaurant", for want of a better word, pushing my plastic food from one side of the plate to the other, I got to thinking about the many times I had argued with my wife. You know, silly little arguments which could have been avoided. At the time I always felt as though I was in the right but looking back - well, it painted a different story. I'm not sure if it's because we're over now. Knowing there is no way back and we're definitely splitting up, I could suddenly see the many errors of my ways. I don't know why I suddenly started to see things from what would have been her point of view. Worse than that, seeing all of the times I'd just been unreasonable flooding back to the forefront of my thoughts. To think, there was once upon a time when I believed I was the perfect partner but - looking back - I was an arse. An idiot.

One time, there was this new film out at the cinema starring Alisha's favourite actor. I don't mind the guy. Usually he plays the "hero" type of character and his films are good fun but - this time - he had come out with a musical. I *hate* musicals and yet here it was, released on the day that we used to make a point of being "cinema-evening". We'd have a meal and then watch a film at the picture house next door. Obviously, she wanted to watch this film. Not just because it was her favourite actor but also because it was a musical and she had a love for those too. She'd also made a point of telling me that I had chosen the film last time. Well - a musical? I told her I would book the tickets and I did but, instead of booking the film she wanted to see - I opted for this new horror sequel instead. Directed by James Wan (aren't they all, these days?), I knew it was a safe booking. Sure his films weren't necessarily original but they were fun. For me anyway. Alisha likes musicals, I like horrors. Anyway - you know where this is going. She wasn't impressed. I shrugged and told her the other film was full. Her reply?

'That's funny. There were plenty of seats when I checked ten minutes ago…'

My reply was fast enough to be convincing, 'Must have been a glitch.'

We didn't argue, I just made sure she had a few glasses of wine with her steak dinner. I knew she wasn't happy though. But yeah, looking back, that was a dick move. The amount of films she'd sat through just to please me and yet I couldn't even watch *one* for her. A relationship is give and take supposedly and yet this wasn't the only example to pop into mind now.

A different dinner date and we were going through the appetisers. Alisha had made a point of saying she wanted the sharer dish of nachos and pulled pork. The waiter came along to take our order and she ordered the nachos. I had to stop the waiter from leaving as he'd presumed it was for both of us but - I'd my heart set on the chicken liver paté. He seemed surprised that Alisha was eating the nachos by herself and - apparently - so was she. At the time though, I'd never said I wanted them too. She just presumed I would share. Anyway that was an issue. Apparently she now looked like a pig and a wasteful one at that.

'You wanted pulled pork and nachos,' I'd told her, 'and they don't have it as a single's dish so... Who's to blame for the waste? You for ordering what you want and only eating your fill or them for not catering for singles.' It had been a fair point on my part, I'd thought.

She'd replied, 'I didn't think I was a single.'

I can see her point now but - at the time - I was adamant that the people in the wrong were actually those who owned the restaurant, not that I'd pointed this out to them. I was too busy enjoying my paté which, by the way, was sublime. My only complaint, again - unvoiced, was that they could have given me a little more toast. Where Alisha had too much on her plate, I didn't have enough. I cleared my plate. She didn't.

'You didn't eat everything so you don't get any dessert,' I'd joked at the time when the plates were being cleared away. It was *this* comment which caused the argument to escalate as she asked why I felt the need to embarrass her like that.

I guess the point I am making is, don't allow yourself to be blinded by your own pig-headedness. Take a step back and try and see the argument from their point of view too. Had I done so myself, I could have probably saved us from numerous disputes or feelings of resentment. Furthermore - we might have still been together. When you go home tonight, don't think back to the past because there's nothing which can be done about it - other than an apology. Just concentrate on the present and how you treat your partner now. Plan for the future, sure, and make those plans nice but… Concentrate on the now before your relationship becomes just a part of your past.

Hindsight is a wonderful thing, hey?

*

'Mr. Charles, did you kill your wife?'

THE TRIP (PART THREE)

5.

Alisha hadn't even bothered to fetch herself a snack from the cupboards at the rear of the camper. This annoyed me more than it should have done because I knew she was just being stubborn now, to prove a point to me. Given the fact we'd only had a small breakfast, I *knew* she'd have been hungry by now. Still - I bite my tongue. The whole point of coming out of the service station was to try and make amends, not to pick a further fight.

She was sitting at the small table, close to the front of the camper, where I'd left her. Damn near made me jump out of my skin when I opened the side door just to see her sitting there staring at me. I closed the door and set my little box of food down on the table. Before taking a seat, I popped the lid off and set that to the side.

'Before I sit down - want me to grab two plates? I went for the big breakfast so - as you can see - plenty to share.' I told her.

I looked down at the sloppy mess in the box. It appeared the "restaurant" was even less fussed about presentation once the food was leaving their establishment. Beans were mixed all over the hash browns and undercooked bacon. The runny egg had burst its yolk and curdled with the bean juice. The only thing which looked remotely edible in the breakfast's current state was the sausage.

'I'd be lying if I said it looked much better when it was on the plate,' I said.

Finally she cracked a smile.

'So - where were you thinking of eating?' I asked.

'I don't see the point in eating out when we purposefully filled the fridge and cupboards with enough food to last us,' she said. She wasn't being shitty. Her tone was - for once - fairly calm. She was also speaking the truth. We *had* spent a fair amount of money on filling the camper van with provisions in order to avoid eating out every day and yet here I was, spending money on terrible food. A few months ago, I would have argued her point by saying we can't be expected to eat in all of the time and why shouldn't we treat ourselves from time to time? She would counter that by simply telling me I was stupid and - in circles we would go.

'Good point,' I told her.

I took a hold of the box of "left-overs" and tossed it directly into the black bin beneath the small sink in the tiny kitchen area of the camper. I could see Alisha in my peripheral vision. She was shaking her head slowly. Before, I would have asked her what her problem was but not now. Not with this "new me" attitude. I simply turned my attention to what we had to eat in the fridge. This is something else the new me is doing. The old me would have sat down and demanded it was only fair that *she* prepared some lunch because *I* had been the one to drive. But not today. Today I was going to do it all.

The contents of the fridge were varied. There were items for a salad, meat based products for sandwiches or frying, pre-boiled eggs the wife had prepared before we left, a pint of milk, various condiments and some yoghurts. I turned back to my wife.

'Is there anything you fancy in particular?' I asked.

'Anything.'

I hate it when she said *anything* in response to such a question. She would say she wasn't fussy and that anything would do until the moment I went to serve up whatever I had chosen. Then she would turn around and act all disappointed and *then* tell me what she really wanted. It was infuriating then and it's infuriating now.

'Come on, there must be something you fancy,' I said with the fridge door wide open.

'Honestly - anything. I'm not even that hungry.'

I sighed. Here I was trying to do the right thing and yet she couldn't even meet me halfway.

I closed the fridge.

'What are you doing?' she asked.

'We can eat when you're hungry. It's fine.'

'You said you were hungry.'

'I ate a bit in the restaurant before I came back out. It'll tide me over until later,' I said.

'Just eat something!'

'It's fine. I've taken the edge off. Might as well hit the road…'

She interrupted me, 'I can't believe you.'

'What?'

'You said you were hungry and…'

I interrupted her, '… and I ate a little in the restaurant. It will tide me over. There is no point in making something for myself if you're not hungry when I can wait a bit and eat something with you, later, when you *are* in the mood to eat.'

Silence.

'Well if I can hungry I can get myself something to eat,' she said.

I bit my tongue despite the swelling frustration within me. By coming back out, I thought I had been doing the right thing. I thought I had been extending an olive branch. I thought I was making this trip a little easier. No. All I've done is given her another way to be as awkward as possible and - to be frank - the temptation to give the trip up and head home was strong.

'We'll eat later,' I said, putting my foot down.

I walked through to the driver's seat and sat down. The keys were still where I'd left them hanging in the ignition.

'You're being ridiculous,' she said.

Again, I bit my tongue. She wants a fight. She is pushing for a fight. I won't give it to her though. I won't let her ruin this trip. To think there was a part of me that thought this could have been a make or break trip. Now I just want it over.

A pity.

CONFUSED

6.

I didn't want to be with her anymore. At least that was what I had thought before we'd left the house. The marriage was over. We weren't right together. We would press one another's buttons and then - when they reacted - we would spark back and, before you knew it, you had a raging fire flaming out of control. We'd both said words and hurtful things from which you can't go back. I mean, I don't need to go into specifics but - even if you did want to try again, you'd always hear the horrible things on those days when you're already feeling low. They'd be there to come back and haunt you. I knew the marriage was over. I knew the trip was nothing more than one final vacation before we got the divorce settled. I even kept telling myself that - if it weren't for the fact we couldn't cancel without losing the money - we probably wouldn't have even gone on the trip...

The thing is, I kept finding myself stealing glances at her now and then. She would just be sitting close to me and my head would turn. She didn't notice though. She just kept staring dead ahead with her eyes fixed to whatever it was that had her attention at that given time. There were times on the trip when I looked at her, hating her. There were times when I looked at her and recalled the good times. Then - like any red-blooded male - there were times when I looked at her and pictured myself inside her. I heard her sighs. I recalled her touch, her scent, her tightness and how wet she'd get for me...

*

'Mr. Charles...'

*

My emotions were all over the place and I was at a point where I didn't know what I wanted anymore. More to the point I didn't know what my wife wanted either. Was she feeling the same? Was she thinking that - actually - with all the good times we'd had over the years, should we really be so quick to throw it away? Was it worth a last-ditch attempt to try and patch things up and make them right again? Or - if we tried - were we just wasting more time and gearing ourselves up for more heartbreak? As it stood, we had both got used to the fact we were over. We had recovered from the heartache caused by the realization that our marriage was doomed. To just open that can of worms again, would we just be lining ourselves up to re-live that pain and misery again? Or - maybe - if we did try and make things work... If they didn't work out... Maybe it would be easier to walk away the second time?

*

'What about your wife?'

I looked blankly at the man sitting opposite me. Both he and his colleague were staring at me. The tape in the recorder was continuing to turn, recording the conversation. Or, in this case, the near silence in the room. The only sound currently audible being the whirring noise coming from the machine.

I clicked my tongue off the roof of my mouth.

'Mr. Charles?' He asked again, 'Did you kill your wife?'

'Are you married?' I glanced down to his left hand which rested on the scratched surface of the table separating us. There was a gold band around his finger. 'Do you and your wife argue?' It was a rhetorical question. Most couples have - at some point - argued. That doesn't necessarily mean the arguments are severe or that they even jeopardise the relationship - but most couples argued at some stage. It is impossible to go a lifetime without a single disagreement. Case in point: If my wife was here with me now, she would disagree with this statement. 'My wife and I argue from time to time. That's it. She'd want something. I wouldn't want it. Or vice versa. That - in turn - would spark a disagreement.' I paused a moment. 'But I don't understand why you keep asking if I killed her when she is alive and well...'

The two men looked at each other and then back to me. I, in turn, looked towards the gentleman sitting to my side who was staring back at the two officers opposite. I turned back to them unsure as to whether this was all some kind of joke. Maybe, the thought crossed my mind, it was a prank and - hidden around the room - there were a number of small cameras ready to capture my panic at the prospect of my wife being deceased. Or - my heart skipped a beat - maybe she is dead and, sitting here now, I'm the number one suspect?

'What's going on?' I asked. 'What's happened to my wife?'

The most talkative of the two men sighed heavily. He said, 'Why don't you tell us about the argument?'

My heart was racing. They had all these questions for me to answer and yet none of them were being quick to answer mine. And they want to know about *the* argument? How do you pick one from many?

THE TRIP (PART FOUR)

7.

Sitting in the front of the camper, travelling down yet another long straight, I couldn't help but to keep glancing in the sun-visor's mirror to Alisha. She hasn't moved from the kitchen area of the camper. Still sulking with me, I guess.

'Did you want to come keep me company?' I asked in the hope she'd say *yes*. Without answering me verbally, she got up and walked through to the front. She took a seat on the passenger side and immediately turned to look out of the window, not that there was much to see.

Curious about her reaction, I reached over to her leg and gently placed my hand on it. She flinched at the initial touch but didn't try and move away and so, I relaxed a little. But just as she didn't flinch, neither did she say anything either.

'You know,' I said cautiously, 'you can talk to me.'

There was a pause.

'And say what?'

'Anything!' Sarcastically I suggested, 'You could talk about the amazing view...'

We were driving down the motorway. The road was long, straight and - thankfully - pretty quiet with regards to the traffic on it. Either side of the motorway there were fields as far as the eyes could see but even those held little to talk about given the fact that only recently whatever had been growing there had recently been harvested.

'You could start suggesting things to do on this trip?' I threw out another suggestion for her, desperate to try and break this stony silence.

'I want to go home,' she said quietly.

I looked at her, momentarily taking my eyes off the road. She didn't return my glance, her eyes still fixed on the world beyond. Without a word, I put my hand back on the steering wheel and pulled over to the hard shoulder. I turned the hazards on before twisting in my seat to face her. She looked at me, tears in her eyes.

'What did you say?' I asked. I knew what she had said. Despite the fact she had mumbled, it was hard not to hear it and - furthermore - it was impossible to mistake it for something else. She didn't repeat what she'd said. I continued, struggling to keep my calm, 'Just over a week, that's how long this trip is. We both agreed to go on it together; one final trip for old time's sake…'

'I…' Whatever she was going to say, she stopped herself.

'I'm trying my best to keep the peace. Not even sure you can tell but… I am. All I ask is that you at least pretend as though you're having a nice time…'

'But…'

I cut her off, 'Do that and - who knows - maybe we'll have a nice trip? Maybe we can go home without feeling as though we have wasted both our time and *my* money?' I paused, curious to see if she had anything to add. The pause turned to silence.

'I'm sorry,' she finally spoke, breaking the silence.

An apology? In all our time together, I never thought I would hear such a thing.

'It's fine,' I told her, trying to be the bigger man and brush all the unpleasantness under the carpet. 'Can we just try and have a nice trip though? That's all I ask.'

She nodded. A single tear rolled down her cheek. I looked at her, confused. How could *that* have upset her? It's not as though I was overly nasty to her. Even when the temptation has been there, to give her a verbal dressing down, I've never gone to my full potential. If anything, she gets off much easier than she sometimes deserves.

I turned the hazards off as I swivelled back around in the driver's seat. Feet on pedals and my hands on the wheel, I glanced to the side mirrors to look for a break in the oncoming cars; a little gap that I could safely pull out of in order to rejoin the motorway. When the coast was clear, I pulled away from the side of the road.

'May I put the radio on?' she asked after a few minutes of silence.

'You know I miss you, right?' I said to her.

My confession was met with silence once more.

'I know we…' I hesitated and just repeated my earlier sentiment, 'I miss you.'

I put my hand back on her leg. For the second time, she didn't pull away. At the same time though, she didn't say she missed me.

To save myself the rejection, I told her, 'You can put the radio on.'

ONE PHONE CALL

8.

'So - what - your wife wanted to go home, you didn't? You got into an argument over it and one thing led to another? Maybe you pushed her and she fell back and hit her head in the sweet spot? Maybe it was an accident? Maybe you knew exactly what you were doing?' The officer paused in his attempts to draw what he must have presumed to be a confession from me.

I couldn't help but to smile, not because I found him funny. I just found the whole situation amusing. Here they were, blaming me for killing my wife when - she isn't dead! Well unless something bad has happened to her whilst I have been away but - even if that is the case, God forbid, I have an alibi. I really *am* innocent of whatever they think I have done.

I said again, 'My wife isn't dead. I don't know why you keep saying that she is.' I turned to my lawyer. 'If you have your phone, we can call her and then you'll all see?'

The lawyer turned to the officers with raised eyebrows - the eyebrows themselves seemingly asking the question *is it okay* on behalf of his mouth.

The leading officer shook his head in disbelief.

'Go right ahead. And then,' he continued, 'perhaps we can stop this pointless dance and just get to the truth?'

'Hopefully,' I said.

The lawyer reached into his jacket pocket and pulled out his phone. Given the fact my battery had long since died, it was - for me - a good job that I could recall her number. I tapped it into the lawyer's handset when he passed it over to me.

'It's ringing,' I said when the phone lines connected.

'Speaker-phone please,' the officer said.

As per the request, I set the handset to speaker and put it upon the table top. We all sat there a moment, listening to the ringing. From the look on the two officers' faces, it was evident to me that they didn't believe anyone would be answering. In fairness, there was a chance Alisha wouldn't answer. She had a habit of screening calls she didn't recognise. When I told her to answer them, she would just tell me that - if it was important - they would leave a voicemail message. Then, when they didn't bother, she'd shrug and say it clearly hadn't been worth answering.

The line clicked.

'Hello,' Alisha's voice came over the speaker.

The look on the officers' faces was priceless and I couldn't help but to smile.

'Baby, it's me...'

'What did I say about calling? You need to stop!'

'I know I'm sorry but it's not what you think... I'm at the police station and there are two officers here who keep asking whether I killed you...'

'What?' There was a sigh. 'You know what - I'm not playing your games anymore. Stop phoning me. We're over!'

Before I could say anything else, the line went dead. I slid the handset back to the lawyer who - without a word - dropped it back into his suit jacket's inner pocket.

Embarrassed by her reaction, I tried to make a joke, 'She loves me really.'

The two men looked at one another. Their confusion was both obvious and also amusing. I sat back in the plastic chair and allowed myself a couple of seconds to enjoy this moment.

I asked, 'So - are we done then?'

The leading officer turned his attention back to me. The confused look in his eyes had gone and back was the glint of hostility which I'd since grown accustomed to. I couldn't help but feel if this situation had been taking place ten years ago, he'd soon be bringing out the telephone book to beat a confession from me as his partner watched on.

'Mr. Charles stop the bullshit. Who was the dead girl you were with?'

I smiled. And there was the question he should have asked at the beginning of the interview. Could have saved himself all this time.

End Of Part One

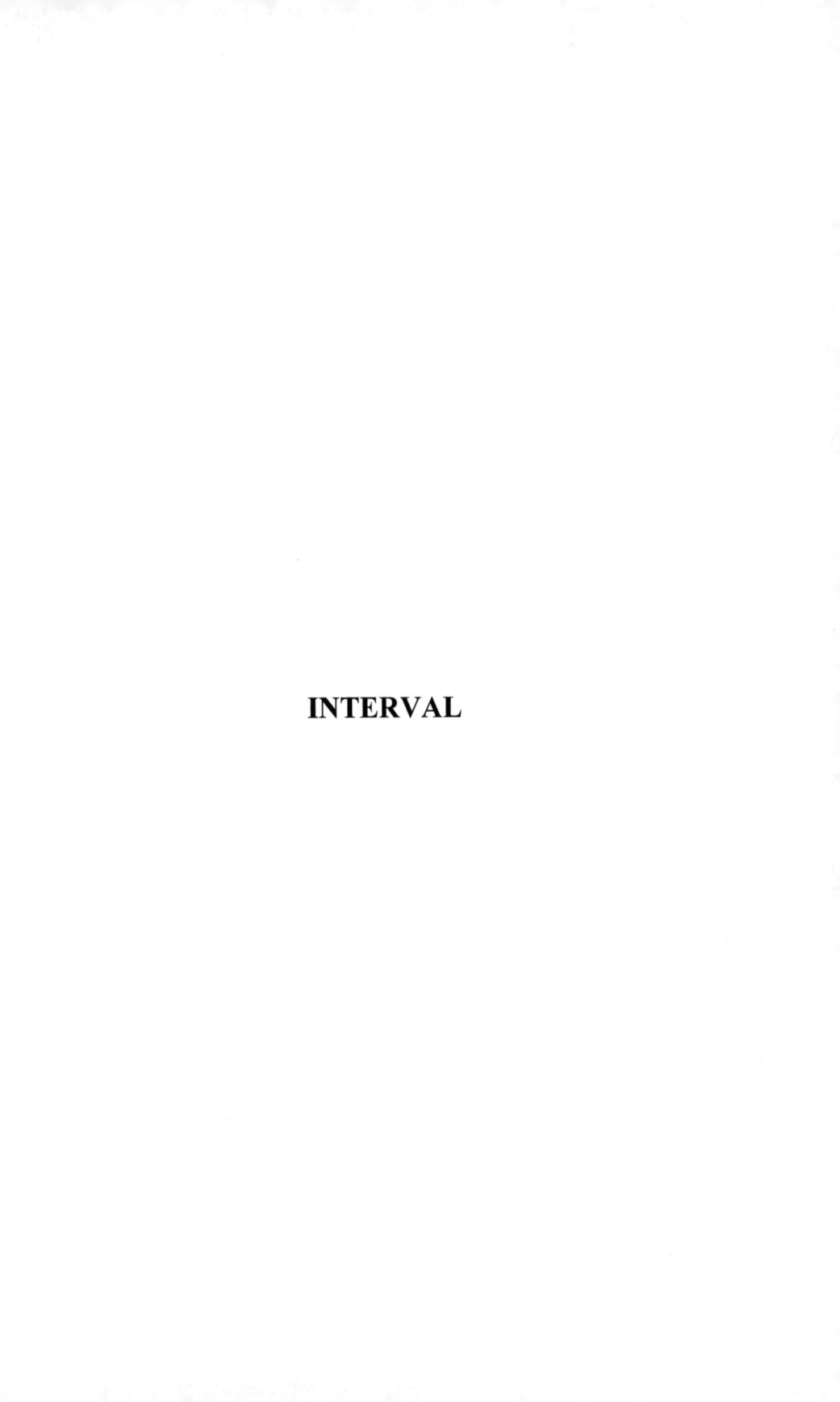

INTERVAL

YOUR NAME IS ALISHA NOW

(BEFORE)

The phone is ringing but she isn't answering. She never answers anymore. The last conversation we'd had being far from friendly despite my best intentions to keep her calm. She'd just shouted at me to leave her alone and that she didn't want to hear from me anymore. She'd called me all the names under the sun, she'd told me how I was the biggest piece of shit going and she was happy where she was now and how *he* made her far happier than I ever had. She mocked me saying that I only noticed her now she was no longer there. She told me that I had done this. She told me I deserved the pain I felt and - then – she ranted about how she would get a restraining order if I didn't stop harassing her. This woman that I used to love.

This woman that I *still* love.

The phone clicked through to her answering service but I didn't bother to leave a message begging her to call me back. She'd had enough messages from me by now and it was obvious she wasn't going to get in touch. I hung the call up and sighed heavily.

I felt sad that she hadn't answered me but I didn't cry. I just put the phone back in my pocket and turned to my guest. My back-up plan.

'We need to colour your hair,' I told her.

She didn't answer me. She just sat there, chained to the radiator. Her eyes were red-raw from all the crying she'd done. No more tears at the moment though. Like me, she was running dry.

Her frame was the same size as Alisha's but her hair colour was off. She was a mousey-blonde and Alisha was a brunette. An easy fix though and I'd already purchased the dye. I walked over to the packet I'd left on the table. Picking it up, I turned it around and read the instructions on the back.

'Do you know how to use this?' I asked.

She shook her head. Looking at her, I'm not sure if she is telling the truth or not. I'm sure, when the time comes, she will soon take charge and put it in her hair to save herself from me making a mess of it. Women are very particular about their hair.

'Well how hard can it be?' I said, filling the awkward silence.

I'd told her about the trip. I'd warned her that if my wife wouldn't come with me, she would have to. Not a replacement to Alisha but, rather, a Plan B. Something which might help me move on, not that I want to but - clearly - Alisha's hoping that's what I do.

'We'll put this in your hair and then get an early night,' I told her. 'Tomorrow, we'll hit the road.'

'Please… I have a son…'

'And if you want to see him again you'll do this trip with me and do as I tell you. Then, when we come back, I'll take you home to your son and you never need see me again.' I added, 'I'm not asking anything strenuous from you. If anything you should thank me…'

'What?'

'It's a free holiday!'

I smiled at her. She didn't smile back.

PART TWO

THE TRIP (PART FIVE)

9.

I didn't like the radio station Alisha had chosen but I suspect she knew that when she leaned down and turned the volume up to a near uncomfortable level. I tried to zone it out, replaying memories of old in my mind's eye as I concentrated upon the road ahead.

I couldn't help but feel disappointed in myself for telling her that I missed her. It was a momentary lapse in concentration and a temporary blindness to the goal at hand.

My Plan B. was simple. I'd told *Alisha* to push me away. As crazy as it sounded, she was to contradict me at every given opportunity. She was to try and bait me into an argument. It might sound stupid but - the point was, by doing this, I would fall out of love with her and eventually drive home with my mind set upon the divorce. Unlike the story's ending with my real wife though, this story would end with the break-up being *my* choice. My decision. Not hers. I was re-writing the truth with a fabricated ending that was easier to swallow down. A pill, if you like, to rid myself of the pain I'd felt.

On this trip, Alisha was doing all that I'd asked. She's refused to eat with me, she's refused to choose somewhere to go... She's been as awkward as possible. She was - for all intents and purposes - perfect and I couldn't have been happier with her performance. The fact I found myself missing her was nothing to do with her acting abilities and drive to get home to her son though. It was my own stupid brain highlighting various ways I pushed her away in the first place. And - how I could have *saved* the marriage instead of watching it burn to a cinder. Putting my hand on her leg was stupid. Telling her that I missed her was worse.

I glanced across to the woman sitting at my side. Despite the fact that she was a few years younger - and so her skin less wrinkled, not that Alisha looked bad or old - she was the spitting image of my wife. Her body was the same shape, her face shape was the same, even her eyes looked similar. And her hair, since we'd dyed it and I'd given it a bit of a trim.

Something clicked in my brain and a little voice spoke up; *maybe it would be easier to get over Alisha's departure if I was with another woman?* The only way forward is to be hand in hand with someone else. Making her look like Alisha was never going to work. Not all the time I love her so much that my chest hurts.

'We need to dye your hair,' I told her.

Alisha turned and looked at me, confused.

'What's your name?' I asked her.

I could see from her face that she wasn't sure whether she should be answering me or not. Perhaps, she thought, this was a test to check that she'd stay in character? Maybe she is worried that - if she fails - I won't let her home to see her son?

'It's okay,' I told her. 'I made a mistake bringing you here.'

'You'll let me go home?'

I quickly corrected myself. 'I made a mistake bringing you here *as my wife*. I thought by having you pretend to be her... I thought by getting you to pretend to push me away… I thought it might help me fall out of love with her. I could forget that she left me for someone else. I could come to terms that I won't see her again… Won't wake up with her each morning or go to bed with her in the evenings. I thought…' I stopped. The woman was looking at me blankly. Her left eye had welled up a little whilst her right remained dry. A single tear spilled down her cheek and dropped onto her top. Her top? One of my wife's tops that she'd left me with - not through choice, she'd just forgotten to take her clothes from the ironing pile. I cleared my throat and continued.

'I should have brought you out as *you*. You know - taken the time to get to know you. The type of person you are, the things you like such as your hobbies and…' I stopped again to save myself from rambling on like a mad man. 'Well - all of that starts with your name.'

From her face I could see that she was still clearly hesitant.

'It's okay,' I reassured her again, 'this isn't a test or anything stupid. I'm not trying to trick you.' I added, 'You can tell me… What's your name?'

EMMA ROBERTS

10.

'Emma Roberts,' I told the officer confidently.

He took out a pen from his inside jacket pocket, along with a little notepad from the same pocket. He flipped it open to the next clear page and jotted her name down with handwriting more suited to a doctor. He closed the pad again before putting both pad and pen back in his pocket.

'And what was your relationship with Emma Roberts?' he asked.

I hesitated. That was a tough question to answer. What *was* my relationship with her? To start off with, she hadn't existed to me. She was Alisha. But then, as the trip went on, she became Emma. Technically I abducted her but... At the stage we got to together... Am I in a position to call her a friend at the very least?

'Did your wife know about her?'

The officer jumped in with another question. I presume he took my silence as a refusal to answer the question as opposed to not actually knowing *how* to answer it. Still - I could answer the latest question.

'No.'

'Were you having an affair? Your wife didn't know about it but Emma grew tired of being *the other woman*? Is that what happened? Did she threaten to tell your wife? You snapped and killed her in a moment's madness in an effort to save your relationship? It's an all too common story. It's one we have heard time and time again...'

'We weren't having an affair.' I suddenly smiled as his words repeated themselves in my head.

'What's so funny?' he asked me.

'You think I killed this woman to save my marriage but... You heard how Alisha was with me on the telephone. She doesn't want to know me. She doesn't want me calling her, talking to her, seeing her... She wants nothing to do with me. And yet - given how she feels about me - you still think I'd kill a woman to stop her finding out I could potentially be seeing someone else. Surely if I was seeing someone else that would mean I'd moved on and I was happy? Why would I care if a woman who hated me found out I was happy now?'

'You'd be surprised some of the stories we hear, and the fucked up motives for murder.' The officer sat back in his chair as the smile slowly faded from my face. 'So you weren't having an affair with this woman but you were travelling around with her? I'll ask again - what was your relationship with her?'

There was a slight pause as I considered my answer.

THE TRIP (PART SIX)

11.

Emma looked uncomfortable sitting opposite me. We'd parked up at the next service station we'd come across and moved the conversation from the front of the camper through to the kitchen area where we sat at the small table. She was on one side, I was on the other. She was sitting on her hands, mine were resting upon the wooden table-top with their palms pressed down.

I'd told her of my new plans: The fact I wanted to get to know her and that I hoped, by doing so, it would help me move on from Alisha. I'd told her that, if she was just *normal* with me now... You know, be herself.... If she did that for me, at the end of the trip, I would still take her home to her waiting child. Basically the same rules for the end of the trip just with a different middle section. Thankfully it didn't take much to explain what I wanted and it was easy for her to grasp what I was saying. Since telling her though, she had gone quiet. Instead of chatting with me, letting me see who she really was, she seemed to withdraw into herself. This was *not* a part of the new plan. I'd pulled into the service area so that we could have further conversations so I could understand what was going on in her head. The key to a good relationship being good communication… Something I which had been missing from my relationship with Alisha. Something which, in the end, drove us apart to the point of there being no return. With that unpleasant past experience so fresh in mind, there was no way I was going to kickstart a new relationship following that very same pattern.

'Are you okay?' I asked her.

She didn't respond.

'This silent treatment doesn't help our relationship,' I added.

She looked at me with what I believed to be a look of disbelief in her tearful eyes.

'It's okay,' I reassured her. 'I'm not mad. You *can* talk to me.'

'Our relationship… That's what you said?'

'I did.'

'But we don't have a relationship. You brought me here against my will. You said you wanted me to act like your wife but in a way that would push you away…'

'That's right.'

'And that - if I did that - you'd take me home when you had to return the camper…'

'Also right.'

'But now you want to get to know me. You want me to be a distraction from your ex-wife…'

'Wife… We aren't divorced.'

Silence.

'I'm sorry,' I told her, 'please continue. Talking is good.'

She looked nervous.

'You told me that you would take me home but if you get to know me… If I am a good distraction…' She stopped talking.

I found myself struggling to not get annoyed with her. There was clearly something on her mind and a point to be made so I wished she'd just spit it out, whatever it was, instead of dragging it on and on. How can I help to fix the issue if she won't even get it out in the first place? When she failed to continue her explanation, I gave her a little nudge.

'I can't help you if you don't tell me what the problem is,' I said.

She cleared her throat in a way I found irritating. Even so, I bit my tongue and waited for her to finish her delayed explanation.

'If you like me,' she said, 'why would you let me go?'

Silence.

'I want to see my son…'

Silence.

'Please, I just want to go home…'

Slowly I tried to explain for fear of panicking her further. 'I want to get to know you because it would mean I am *capable* of getting to know someone else without thoughts of Alisha holding me back. I want to get to know you to help me move on from my wife, yes. If I develop feelings for you? Well that depends on how you feel for me. What if you develop feelings for me and I didn't have any for you? You'd be just as hurt as I would be but - doesn't mean it wouldn't be possible to move on. At this stage of our relationship we are nothing but friends and so - if one has feelings for the other and the other person doesn't feel the same... You move on. I'm only struggling now, with Alisha, because we have been together for so long. Had I met her and fancied her, and she hadn't fancied me... I would have simply moved on. Would it have hurt? Probably. But it is a different kind of hurt. Do you understand?'

'You won't kill me?'

I looked at her in shock. This woman, sitting opposite me, how could she think I wanted to kill her? I'm not a murderer.

'I don't want to kill you.'

'You abducted me.'

'I wanted your help. I promised to take you home and I will.'

Silence.

I added, 'And what if you like me by the end of the trip and I like you too? Sure it wouldn't have been the most normal way to start a relationship - in fact we'd probably be better off lying about how we met if people asked - but, it's possible? What if this is actually the start of something special? You mention your child a lot but you never mention another half so I am guessing you're a single parent?'

A slight hesitation before she answered, 'I am.'

'So what if we fell for each other? At this stage - we don't know what is going to happen. I'm just a normal guy, sitting opposite a woman I find beautiful, asking permission to get to know her. Is that so bad? And, like I said, at the end of the trip - you go home to your son and I go home to my life.' I shrugged. 'I can't say what happens after that. I mean I might find you a nice person on this trip but it doesn't mean I would want to be with you. Flip side of that coin, I might really enjoy your company and you may want nothing more to do with me in which case - you won't see me again. Then, of course, there is always the possibility we like each other and want to see where it goes…'

She is looking at me with a blank expression on her face.

I asked, 'Do you even understand?'

She nodded.

I leaned across and wiped a stray tear from her cheek. I smiled at her. 'You're so pretty,' I said. She - in turn - forced a smile back. It was a good start. 'Ready to hit the road again?'

Again, she nodded.

COMPLICATED

12.

I liked Emma. She was a nice girl with - seemingly - a good heart. But how does one define the relationship we had? I don't know how she felt about me.

'Mr. Charles?'

I snapped back to reality unaware I'd even zoned out in the first place. The two men were looking at me, awaiting an answer to their question; the one I was struggling with. I looked at them blankly and shrugged.

'You don't know what your relationship was?'

'It was complicated.'

'Complicated?'

'Yes.'

'How so?'

'I liked her. She was a nice girl.'

'What? She didn't like you? You wanted more than she was prepared to give and so you killed her? If you couldn't have her, no one could?'

'I didn't say that.' I added, 'I said it was complicated. I knew what I thought of her. She was a nice girl. She was pleasant to talk to, when she spoke. She was good to look at. She seemed as though she could be my *type*. Were we boyfriend and girlfriend though? No. Were we even friends? Well - I would like to think so but I couldn't say for sure. So, given the circumstances, if you were sitting here and I was asking you the questions... How would you answer it?'

The man looked at me with a smug look on his face.

'I wouldn't be sitting that side of the table,' he told me.

We sat for a moment with the silence broken only by the whirring of the tape machine recording our conversation.

'So you liked her?' the officer asked eventually.

'I did.'

He smiled.

I couldn't help myself and asked, 'Why are you smiling?'

'Because you tell us you liked her…'

'I did.' I corrected myself, 'I do.'

'And you would have been happy for her to call you a friend?'

'Of course.'

'So then - why did you kill her?' He added, 'When I have friends or acquaintances, I tend to keep them close to me. They're good for talking to, nights out… Anything really. I don't think about killing them.'

I shook my head again. He was really so cock-sure that I had killed her but I hadn't. I might have been caught with her body but her death wasn't on my hands although I knew - even if I said that to him - the officers wouldn't believe me.

'So what did she do that was so bad?' he asked, pushing for a confession that I couldn't give.

'What makes you think she did anything?' I asked.

THE TRIP (PART SEVEN)

13.

We had been driving for a couple of hours now. Day had turned to darkness part illuminated only by the camper's lights. Occasionally extra light was offered by oncoming traffic.

Despite our conversation at the table, Emma still wasn't really opening up to me. I would occasionally look over to where she was sitting next to me but her eyes would be fixed dead ahead. There were other times - like now - where I'd look over and she'd appear as though she was sleeping. There was a suspicious part of my character which wondered whether she really was asleep or whether she was merely pretending.

Tunes played quietly over the vehicle's stereo. They were barely audible but enough to kill the silence and drown out the sound of the tyres on the road's un-smooth surface.

Feeling tired, I turned off the motorway at the next junction. The exit led up a slight hill towards a roundabout. To the left was a single lane - trees either side. Straight ahead - the opportunity to re-join the motorway. To the right, a bridge over the motorway we'd been on, a route to re-join it but heading in the opposite direction - back the way we'd come from. I turned left.

The road was long and straight, similar to the ones I'd already driven down. I miss the country roads close to where I live; they have a few straights but long sweeping corners. The time spent racing faster than I should have been, back when I was much younger, were some of the happiest summer evenings of my life. Windows down, music blaring - I was the master of the road. Nowadays everywhere I seem to drive is like this; long, dull… No wonder people fall asleep at the wheel. There's no reason for them to keep their eyes open. Still, hopefully there will be somewhere off-road where we can pull in for the evening. Speaking of people falling asleep, I'm struggling to stay awake now. The hours of driving, mixed with my flowing emotions, seems to have taken it out of me. I looked at Emma sleeping to my side and I felt a pang of jealousy, even though she didn't exactly look comfortable.

The radio started to crackle as the signal grew weaker. That would be the third radio station I'd lost since leaving my home. With one hand on the wheel, one eye on the road, I leaned down to the radio and started scrolling back through the stations. Most were static with the only one accessible being some kind of late night chat show whose host appeared to have the dullest of voices. Still, it was better than the sound of static. Just.

As my full attention went back to the road, I noticed a turn-off into an extended lay-by intended to be used by trucks as a rest-point. It wasn't ideal but it was better than nothing so - with no need to indicate due to the lack of traffic - I turned off the road and pulled the camper to a stop. No sooner had I done so, I killed both the engine and the lights plunging us into near darkness.

'Where are we?'

My movement had woken Emma from her slumber.

'Home for the night,' I told her. I smiled. 'I got tired and needed to pull over. Not much to look at or do but - soon as I've gotten my head down for a little bit - we'll hit the road again.'

Emma squinted into the darkness. I'm unsure of what she'd hoped to see out there.

I reassured her, 'It won't always be like this. Some places will be proper rest-stops or camping sites. Just feels like I have been driving forever with no opportunities but this…' I smiled at her. 'I'll do for this evening. Right?'

She nodded.

I undid my seat-belt and got up from the seat before walking through to the back of the van. There was a double bed set up at the rear of the camper, hidden behind a hanging curtain. I moved the curtain to one side and looked at the bed. Given how we are technically "friends" now, as opposed to husband and wife, I'm unsure on the protocol for sleeping arrangements.

I heard Emma enter the space directly behind me and felt sure she would be thinking the same thing.

'You can have the bed,' I told her. I turned to face her and - indeed - her eyes were fixed on the sleeping space. 'We'll put the curtain across and I'll sleep on the floor.'

There wasn't much space on the floor to roll around but at least there'd be enough to fully stretch my six foot two frame out. It would be no worse than sleeping in a sleeping bag.

'Thank you,' she said quietly.

I smiled. 'My pleasure.'

I glanced over to the kettle on the side where it was secured in place to stop it sliding around on the kitchen work-top.

'When I go to bed, I like to have a hot drink. I find that it helps me sleep better.' I walked over to the kettle and loosened the fastenings so that I could fill it with water. 'Would you like one?' I asked.

She hesitated a moment. 'Yes, please.'

'Got coffee, tea or even chocolate.' I added, 'I fancy some chocolate myself. That good with you?'

She nodded.

'Well then,' I continued, 'take a seat. I'll get the drinks.'

I started to prepare the drinks, taking the hot chocolate sachets from the cupboard and the mugs from where they were kept - also secured so as not to slide around and potentially break.

'Do you mind if we open the door to let some air in?' she asked.

I looked at the closed door a few feet away from me and then at her. She'd been good at the service station, not trying to signal for help or run from me - no doubt scared I'd do something to her child as originally promised. I was sure I could trust her now too. Especially given we are so far from civilisation. Where was she going to go?

'Sure.' I added, 'But if too many bugs start coming in, we'll have to close it again. Nothing worse than mosquitos...'

'Okay.'

I gestured for her to open the door for herself and turned my back to her as she got up to do just that. I poured one of the chocolate sachets into the first mug and then another into the second as she - door now open

- took her seat once again. A soft breeze whispered into the stuffy van.

THE WRONG QUESTIONS

14.

'So you were the perfect host?' The officer added, 'As perfect a host can be after abducting someone, that is?'

'I was polite,' I said.

'And yet you still ended up killing a girl.'

'You keep saying that but you don't let me get to the end of my story…'

'Because I am sick and tired of your bullshit. I am sick and tired of listening to what you have to say…'

'Then how do you expect to learn the truth if you are fed up hearing it?'

'When we caught up with you, you told us she was your wife…'

I shrugged. 'I was in shock. About everything.'

'In shock?'

'Yes.'

'Or you were worried because you'd realised you'd just lost all chance of your freedom? So what was the plan anyway? Drive into the middle of nowhere and find somewhere secluded before dumping the body?'

'No. My plan was to get to know the girl. I already told you that.'

'Hard to get to know someone when they're dead. Or, in your sick mind, were you making her talk? You know, acting out her role so you'd ask a question in your voice and then answer it in *her* voice...'

'I'm not insane.'

'An insane person would say that but - truthfully - I hope you're not. If you are, you'd just end up in a secure hospital and - well - I don't want that. I want you to rot behind bars in a proper prison with the real criminals. The people who tend not to take kindly to folk like you killing women...'

'I'm not sure what I find funnier,' I said, 'the fact there are prisoners with morals as to right and wrong or the fact you seem so frustrated that you can't do what you *really* want to do to me. Look at you, Mr. Law... High and Mighty.... Yet it's obvious from your tone and the way you're talking to me that you want to inflict pain on me.'

'I do want to. But I don't. That's the difference between you and me. I want to hurt you but I do my job instead so that you can't hurt anyone else. You, on the other hand, don't care about people and have no qualms about causing death and destruction.'

I frowned at him. He was entirely wrong.

'Death and destruction?'

'That's right. You killed someone and you destroyed their child… They don't know it yet but they will when they find their mother's life was snuffed out by you.'

I shook my head again.

'The only thing I destroyed was my marriage.'

'What - Emma Roberts' life was meaningless?'

'You keep saying I killed her. You keep wanting to know what happened but I never killed her. I told you that but you don't listen. I told you, I liked her.'

'And yet you were caught with her body in your vehicle.'

'The question you need to ask is *who* killed her.'

'I know who killed her. I'm looking at her murderer.'

'But you're not. Her murderer is out there though.'

The officer's face flushed red as he slammed his clenched fist down onto the table. 'Just cut the fucking bullshit and tell us what happened!'

I smiled calmly. 'I'm trying. You keep interrupting me.'

There was silence.

The tape machine continued to whir.

THE TRIP (PART EIGHT)

15.

Emma was quicker than I could have anticipated, diving out of the side door the moment my back was turned. At first - given how we had been chatting - I thought she was joking around but soon realised she was serious and making a break for the freedom I'd always promised her at the end of the trip.

I dropped the held mug to the floor as I ran out after her. It shattered but that was the least of my concerns as I looked left first and then right, just catching sight of her foot disappearing around the back of the camper.

'Wait!' I called out despite knowing she wouldn't.

I followed her and turned the corner in time to hear the tyres of an incoming car screeching over the hard concrete. The dreadful noise - hard to ever imagine forgetting - was accompanied by Emma's scream... A scream cut short, replaced by a metallic sounding thud as she bounced off the car's bonnet and another thud as she landed, hard, upon the tarmac, motionless. The car was also motionless. The brake lights on and illuminating my path towards the scene of the accident.

'What have you done?' I called out. My heart was racing and adrenaline flowing. 'What have you fucking done?!' My question could have been answered by both Emma and the driver: Both were to blame for this.

The driver gave no answer. The brake lights disappeared as the driver's foot must have come off the pedal and, then, the car wheel-span away from the scene leaving me and Emma in near darkness. The only light now, offered up by the overhead moon illuminating the landscape and her broken body.

Emma's arm was twisted at a horrific angle. Even in this poor light I noticed the bone jutting from the back of her elbow. Her legs were seemingly okay but her face was cut up down the side closest to the ground.

'What have you done?' I said again, this time the question more pointed at her. She didn't answer. She couldn't answer.

Her eyes were fixed to a point somewhere over my shoulder. Her mouth was slightly agape.

'What have you done?'

Leaning over her, I reached with shaking hand to her neck. Using two fingers I pressed them against her neck and held my own breath as I waited to feel what turned out to be a non-existent pulse.

She was gone.

I'm not sure if it had been the initial impact by the car, or the severity with which her head hit the tarmac which robbed her of life.

I resumed breathing.

'What have you fucking done…'

Suddenly aware that I was in the middle of a road and that another car may come, I scooped her up in my arms. As I lifted her from the cold, hard ground there was another cracking from her arm which made my blood run cold. There was no time to worry about that thought, or let it affect me. The girl might not have looked as though she'd weigh much but she was heavier than I'd expected. I struggled to get her back to the relative privacy of our camper without dropping her but, when I did, I laid her upon the bed before closing (and locking) the door.

I slumped down on the seat next to the kitchen table, unable to take my eyes from her still body. Her gaze now fixed on the wall at her side. The angle of her head suggesting a broken bone within her neck.

'What have you done?' I muttered again under my breath despite knowing there'd be no answer. I guess I spoke out loud just to kill the uncomfortable silence... Just to take away the deathly stillness that haunted the space we occupied. 'What have you done...'

With only enough warning to get me to the sink, I vomited my stomach contents up into the plastic bowl. A heavy mixture of bile and the remnants of the shitty all-day-breakfast I'd half eaten and a bitter aftertaste that made it hard not to regurgitate for a second time. I closed my eyes to both the horror on the bed and the mess in the sink and sat back down on the seat I'd just vacated. With my eyes closed, I kept seeing the accident replay itself over and over and over...

'What have you done?' I asked the corpse again. 'WHAT HAVE YOU DONE?!'

Not wanting to see the truth of the situation, keeping my eyes closed, I stood up and walked over to the curtain hanging from the camper's roof. I pulled it across, hiding Emma's body from my sight. Out of sight, out of mind.

DISBELIEF

16.

The officers were looking at me as though they didn't believe me. It didn't matter what they thought though, it was the truth. The only way you could say that I killed the woman was by saying it was my fault as, without me, she would never have been there. I guess there is some truth in that. Had I not *borrowed* her, she would still be alive. She'd be at home, with her son, doing whatever it was they did together. But I didn't kill her myself though. I wasn't to blame for her lack of breath. In this instance, I'm not entirely sure who was to blame. She had run out of the camper van, she had run into the road, she had run into the path of an oncoming car... The driver didn't do enough to avoid her and had ended up striking her but... Who was to blame? Is it my fault for taking her there, her fault for running into the road, the driver's fault for not braking in time? Whatever. It was evident from their faces that they didn't believe me.

'Someone hit her and drove off, is that correct?'

'Yes.'

'So that would be a hit and run.'

'If she was struck by an automobile, why didn't you call the police there and then?'

'And say what exactly? The girl I abducted was just hit by a car as she tried to run away from me?'

'I don't think there was an accident. I think you killed her.'

'I didn't.'

'The autopsy report will speak volumes.'

'I didn't kill her.'

'I think you killed her and were looking for somewhere to dump the body.'

'I had no intention of dumping the body.'

'No?'

'No.'

'What junction did this accident happen on?'

'I don't remember. I was driving in an area I am unfamiliar with and...'

'You don't remember?'

'No.'

'Convenient. See, if you could tell us what junction it was - we could check to see if there are any cameras. More than that, there'd be signs of the collision. You said you heard the car tyres screeching... There'd be tyre marks. There'd most likely be blood on the road and parts of the car that struck her too...'

'Give me a map and I might be able to pin point...'

'I don't think there was an accident,' the officer said again, cutting me off once more. 'You killed her,' he said accusingly, 'and you were looking for somewhere to hide the body.'

'That isn't what happened.'

The officer snorted through his nose. It was a strange sound and one which made me want to lean across and smack him in the face right there and then. The only reason I didn't was because - despite what they thought of me - I wasn't a violent man. To date I have never raised a fist to anyone in all my life and I'm not about to change that now just because of the way he was pressing my buttons.

'So - what - you just planned on driving around with her forever?'

I shrugged.

'So how did you go from watching her die to *just driving around with her with no intention of dumping her*...' I could tell by the tone in his voice that he was mocking me.

Again, I resisted the urge to lean across the table and smack him directly in the face. We had come so far with the story now that I just wanted it over and done with so I could go back to the cell they'd dragged me from. I knew I was going to be charged with her abduction anyway and I knew they weren't going to believe my story so - now - I just wanted it done and dusted so I could argue it out in front of a jury instead. This man - maybe even his colleague too - had already made his mind up.

THE TRIP (PART NINE)

17.

Shock had set in and I'd driven many miles and hours before I'd even realised what I was doing. I should have been thankful that I hadn't had an accident whilst I was spaced out but - in truth - it would most likely have been easier if I had. A quick death, diving through a windscreen, as opposed to having to deal with the mess that I'd found myself in. Only now was I beginning to realise what I had done and how far my love for Alisha had brought me down the wrong path. Before this moment, before the dead girl lying in the back of the camper... Everything had seemed so *normal* to me. My fragile - potentially broken - mind somehow having convinced myself that it was okay to take this woman from a life she knew and drive her around the country with there being no repercussions. I could just take her home at the end of it and let her go back to her life whilst I went back to mine - cured of my desires to want to be with Alisha and ready to face the world whilst seeking new love. There was never going to be a happy ending. There was always going to be involvement from the law and now... Their involvement would be so much more severe than before. I had a death on my hands.

I pulled to the side of the road and started to weep. The tears were slow at first but - soon - were flowing freely as I struggled to keep my emotions in check. Tears for Emma, tears for my failed relationship, tears for the fact I knew I'd end my days in a prison, tears for being so pathetic and stupid.

After the accident I'd been shouting at the corpse, demanding to know what she'd done but I should have been asking myself the same question. What had *I* done. I had ruined her life, I'd ruined my life and - before - I'd ruined my wife's life too.

Another question in mind: Why couldn't I have had an accident whilst driving from the scene of the accident to where I was now? It would have made everything so much simpler.

I looked at the road before me. It stretched for miles, further than the eye could see. Any other day, any other situation, I would have found myself wondering where it led but not today. Today I knew it led nowhere. I knew it was a dead end.

'It doesn't have to be.'

Emma's voice came from the back of the camper. I knew it was impossible. There was no way she was alive, just having been *stunned* this whole time. She was dead. I closed my eyes and pretended I hadn't heard her.

'It doesn't have to be a dead end,' her voice said again. This time it was louder. It was clearer. It was harder to ignore. I opened my eyes and twisted round to look at her. She was looking straight back at me.

'It doesn't?' I turned back, front forwarding in my seat. 'How does it not have to be a dead end? Where else can it lead?' I asked her.

'Wherever you want it to.'

THE VOICES

18.

I had been momentarily left in the room and the tape deck was no longer recording. My lawyer had stepped outside for a smoke and the two officers had gone off to talk to someone after the interview had been interrupted by a knock at the door.

I turned my head to look towards the mirror along the far wall. I wondered whether there were any more officers standing upon the other side, listening to the story I had to tell, or whether I was truly alone.

I think they believe I am looking for an insanity plea. Their faces when I told them I had heard Emma talk to me, despite knowing she was dead, suggested they - again - didn't believe me and thought, instead, that I was trying to work the system for an easier life. That's not the case though. I know I wasn't really hearing her voice. I know she wasn't telling me to really push forward and keep on driving with her. I know she wasn't hinting that was the way to avoid my life being flushed away for all I had done wrong. I'm not stupid and I'm not insane. At the time though, it *had* felt real whether people want to believe me or not. It had felt as though she was really talking to me even though I knew it was impossible. If I had to hazard a guess as to why it felt so real, I would blame it upon the shock of the whole situation I had found myself in. The shock, along with the stress and even the fact that I was overly tired. The point of stopping in the first place was to rest and - as it was - I ended up getting no rest whatsoever. Instead, I ended up driving and driving until I finally snapped back to the reality in which she was alive and talking.

I paused a moment recounting all of this in my mind. How do you explain this to someone else? Even now I know it makes very little sense. I know I sound like I've lost my mind but…

I looked up. The two officers had come back in with a beige file in their hands. Their expression gave nothing away. They took a seat opposite me and the talkative officer set the file down in the middle of the table.

'We'll just wait for Mr. Stephens to come back in,' he said, 'and then we'll resume the interview.'

I nodded. Mr. Stephens was the lawyer they'd appointed to my case.

'You know this would all go so much smoother if you'd just tell us the truth,' the officer said.

'I am,' I told him.

He raised his eyebrows as if to say, *really?* He didn't say anything else. There was little point given that my lawyer was missing and that the tape deck hadn't been set back up to record.

It was a few minutes before Mr. Stephens walked back in. Upon noticing us waiting for him, he apologised and promptly took his seat. The officer opposite me pressed "record" on the tape machine and re-introduced the case for the benefit of the recording.

'We have a preliminary coroner's report come back and thought you might like to shed some light on the contents,' he said.

'Which are?' It was hard to shed light on anything when I myself was being kept in the dark.

'There were some vaginal tears and some bodily fluid inside her. The tears suggest there was forced intercourse…' The officer continued, 'Are you sure you didn't kill her? You made your advances, she turned you down and you went ahead anyway? You forced yourself upon her and - knowing she'd report you to the police - killed her to keep her quiet. You were found with her body because you were looking for that perfect spot to hide her. Somewhere she wouldn't be found. Somewhere that'd ensure you'd get away with your…' He stopped talking, no doubt put off by the fact that I was busy laughing at him. Not a little "titter" of a laughter either, but a proper belly laugh. He asked me, 'May I ask what is so amusing?'

'Just what you're saying…'

'That's funny? We're talking about the rape - and murder - of an innocent woman and you find that funny? Most people I've had in your position before now have tended to suddenly find themselves remorseful at this point…'

'It's not funny because she is dead. It's just funny - and this is a bit sick… It's just funny that I kind of *wish* that was what had happened. It's almost better than the truth.'

I managed to compose myself as the officer leaned forward in his chair with his arms crossed before him.

'Care to explain what you mean?' he asked.

THE TRIP (PART TEN)

19.

'It doesn't have to be a dead end,' her voice said again. This time it was louder. It was clearer. It was harder to ignore. I opened my eyes and twisted round to look at her. She was looking straight back at me.

'It doesn't?' I turned back, front forwarding in my seat. 'How does it not have to be a dead end? Where else can it lead?' I asked her.

'Wherever you want it to.'

I hadn't expected the answer. I expected silence but - strangely enough - I was pleased that she *had* answered me.

'Wherever you want us to go,' she continued.

'Us?' I said with a skip in my heart.

'Us.'

Slowly I turned back around in my seat. She was sitting up on the bed. A smile on her face.

'You mean it?' I asked.

She nodded.

I got up from my seat as she patted the bed next to her. Nervously, my heart racing, I walked over. In my head there was a little voice that was screaming how crazy all this was but, a louder voice yelled to drown it out. *The only way out of this mess is to go along with what she was suggesting. Everything that she was suggesting.*

'I'm sorry I tried to run,' she said.

'I'm sorry I hadn't been able to save you…'

'Ssh,' she shushed me quiet. 'It's not your fault. Had I not tried to run, I would never have been hit…'

'But had I not brought you here…'

'I'm glad you did though.'

'You are?'

'If you hadn't. We would never have met.' She continued, 'I actually felt bad that you wanted me to pretend I was Alisha. I felt horrible pretending to push you away so that you could find some kind of closure…'

'You did?'

I was so confused. My head was spinning.

'I did. I wanted you to get to know me just as I wanted to get to know you more for myself.'

'Really?'

'Kiss me.'

'What?'

'You heard me.'

'I'm just…'

'Kiss me,' she said again.

I froze, unsure of what was happening and why. Everything was moving so fast and my head was spinning whilst my mind raced at a million miles per hour.

'Don't overthink it,' she said, 'just kiss me.'

I leaned towards her, waiting, and I kissed her. At first it was a gentle peck on her mouth. She didn't pull away. I kissed her again, this time leaving my lips lingering upon hers. Still she wasn't the first to pull away.

After the embrace, she said, 'I just wish we'd met differently. I wish you'd approached me in a store, or something. Said that you liked the look of me or just asked me out... Everything could have been so...'

I quietened her with another kiss. This time, my tongue pushed inside her mouth and touched upon her tongue. It was drier than I had imagined. As we kissed I couldn't help but run my hands down the side of her body and over her hips. She has the perfect hourglass figure. There is nothing sexier than a woman who's proud of her curves.

I pulled away, if only for air, but my gaze stayed firmly upon hers. All this time with her, the plan of making her act like Alisha and to push me away... So stupid... Time wasted from getting to actually know someone who had the potential to distract me from my failed marriage without having to go through some sort of extensive role-play scenario...

'Fuck I need you inside me,' she said.

I pulled a little further away from her.

'Really?'

'I want you to fuck me...'

I didn't need to be asked twice. I laid her back on the bed gently and pulled the black tracksuit bottoms down.

They originally belonged to Alisha - one of the items of clothing she'd failed to get from the ironing pile. It was the same story for the white jumper Emma was wearing, all a part of making her look more like Alisha. Foolish. Emma's own dress sense, remembering what she'd looked like when I first saw her, was much better. Certainly sexier.

Beneath the tracksuit bottoms were red french knickers. These were her own and had been tainted by her untimely death but - it didn't put me off from wanting to give her the satisfaction she asked for. I pulled them off too and dropped them to the floor where they landed next to the tracksuit bottoms. Then I froze. I was mesmerised by her pussy. Her labia was tidy giving the impression of there being a perfect slit between her legs. This wasn't the same as Alisha. Alisha's lips hung ever-so-slightly, not that I found this to be unattractive. I had just gotten so used to seeing this sort of vagina that I'd forgotten how they can all look different. And - how they can taste different…

From dropping the french knickers to the floor, I kissed my way up her body with my eyes fixed on the final destination of her succulent slit. My heart racing and cock throbbing at the anticipation of what she'd taste like when I did get there.

She laid there, motionless, letting me do as I pleased but no doubt eager for the teasing to stop and my tongue to start exploring her pussy - both inside and out with accompanying nibbles of her clit.

'No,' she said as my mouth moved ever closer to her pussy.

'No?'

'I haven't had a shower. Just... Fuck me...'

Despite the desire to bury my face between her legs to taste all that was on offer, I kissed my way past her pussy and up her cold body until we were face to face.

'You're so beautiful,' I told her.

'Thank you.' She giggled.

I freed my cock from the confines of my jeans and then spat into my hand. I rubbed my saliva onto the head of my cock.

She laughed. 'Mmm, sexy.'

'Sorry.'

It wasn't the sexiest things for her to see and - in hindsight - I should have lubricated my shaft when not face to face with her. Even so - given the circumstances - it was a necessary evil.

'Kiss me,' she said.

I kissed her on the lips and - for a second time that day - pushed my tongue 'tween her parted lips. As I did so, using the same hand I'd used to lubricate myself, I guided my hard-on between her other lips, pushing as deep into her tight vagina as I could. She felt amazing, certainly different to Alisha who felt amazing in other ways… Emma's cunt was so tight around my shaft and after the first few thrusts, I thought I was going to shoot my load before I'd had the chance to do anything but tease her towards an orgasm which wouldn't come unless I managed to last a little longer.

'Don't you cum yet,' she warned me, as though she was reading my mind.

'You're so fucking tight.' I sighed as I started to build a momentum.

'Harder,' she said as she bucked back against my thrusts.

LOST FOR WORDS

20.

I stopped talking when I saw the look on their faces. The officers were just staring. One had his mouth slightly agape and the other was just motionless. Both were seemingly lost for words.

'I didn't rape her,' I said eventually.

'Did she give consent?' the officer asked.

'When a person dies, they lose their status as a person. You can't call sex with a dead body "rape" because rape implies that there is a victim which, in turn, implies the assignment of personhood to a corpse.'

The officer looked at me, stunned.

'I didn't rape her,' I said.

Silence.

'But I did have sex with her.'

'And you thought that was acceptable.'

'At the time I wasn't thinking much. I was hearing her talk to me. I had her consent in my mind. I know - looking back, as I talk to you now, that wasn't the case and that she wasn't talking and…'

'Now? You only *now* realise that wasn't the case? There wasn't a time when you were with her that you realised what you were doing?'

I paused a moment as the two men gave each other a casual glance. I knew what they were thinking.

'I'm not insane and nor am I trying to get a plea of insanity… You're asking me what happened. I'm telling you. You asked if I killed her. I didn't. You asked if I raped her, I didn't.'

'So you just abducted her and then defiled her corpse?' The officer jumped on my words with venom in his voice designed to hurt.

The tape recorder whirred around, capturing all.

'I don't know what else you want me to say,' I said.

'We have come this far, please… Just carry on…' There was a level of sarcasm in the officer's voice which hadn't gone unnoticed. I ignored it and pushed forward with the story.

'You asked as to whether there was a time whilst I was with her when I realised what I was doing…'

'I did.'

'Well, there was.'

The officer sat back in his chair with a not-so-subtle glance at the clock hanging on the wall. No doubt he was curious as to how long we had been in this room for now. He was also most likely fully aware that he only had x amount of hours to charge me with a crime.

I took a sip of the water and cleared my throat.

THE TRIP (PART ELEVEN)

21.

I was unable to hold myself back any longer as I felt the familiar - and pleasant - tingling of an orgasm building up. A great feeling which seemed to build-up from the toes and grow in intensity as it reached my testicles. No doubt more intense thanks to both my partner's tight pussy and for how long it had been since I'd been inside a woman.

The rest of the orgasm came too fast and I was able to give no warning but rather just to let out a loud sigh as I ejaculated inside her. She looked me dead in the eyes as I did so and - the moment I was spent - I realised she wasn't moaning back, as previously heard, and nor was she bucking my hips in time with my thrusts. She was motionless. She was dead. I don't know... I *knew* she was dead but had somehow convinced myself that this wasn't the case. Again, I can but only blame the stress of the situation I was in. A temporary moment of madness maybe? At this particular moment though, the truth came crashing back to me, pulling me down into the harsh reality with a heavy bump.

I immediately pulled out and fell back, off the bed and onto the floor as her pussy let out the air I'd pushed inside - along with a dribble of my ejaculate which bubbled into a pool on the duvet beneath her. I got up and turned my back on what I'd done. An orgasm would usually calm me but now - I felt anything but serenity and *that* question came back to the forefront of my mind.

What had I done?

'You've done nothing,' she said. 'We're just two people in love with one another. Is that such a bad thing?'

'People won't understand.'

'Does it matter what they think?'

'They'll try and stop us from seeing each other.'

'If they find out about us.'

'They will…'

'Not if you just keep driving.'

'And go where?'

'A road with no end. Just keep driving.'

Without looking back, I got up from the floor and made my way to the front of the camper. I made myself comfortable and twisted the key in the ignition. With no plans on where I was going to go, I carefully pulled away.

'We'll need to get some fuel,' I called back.

When we were driving everything was fine. She would talk to me, seemingly in an attempt to get to know me better. She'd ask me about my life, my hobbies... Everything really and - you know - it was nice. The type of conversation that Alisha and I lost long ago. The only times I felt uncomfortable was when we were stuck in non-moving traffic or I'd have to fill the camper up with petrol.

Both occasions, I was stressed that someone would look in and see Emma sitting there. I'd worry that they'd call the authorities or just stand there, screaming - bringing more attention to us when all we wanted was to be left alone. One of the good things about that camper though was the miles per gallon you got from the tank and, with regards to the traffic, we stuck to the quieter country roads as much as possible. With no end destination in mind - it didn't matter that the winding country roads would take a little longer to get from point to point. We weren't in a hurry. No one was waiting for us...

DEAD END

22.

'But there was someone waiting for you,' the officer said, interrupting my story. 'The rental company,' he added.

I didn't say anything. There was nothing to say; he was right. I'd only rented the camper. Of course they were going to report it as stolen when I failed to return it, and - worse - ignored their calls. Had I been thinking straight, I could have extended the rental maybe? They might have taken a payment over the phone? I don't know. I hadn't been thinking straight, as I kept saying.

With the camper reported as stolen, it wasn't long before I was pulled over and the rest - they say - is history. The never-ending road Emma and I had imagined had reached a dead end.

The officer looked at me with a smug look on his face.

'You probably thought you were committing the perfect crime,' he suggested.

I looked at him, at him and his colleague, and tried now to laugh. I never intended to set out and commit any crimes, as crazy as that sounds with my story now laid out upon the table - captured forever by the ever-recording tapes. I only tried to cure myself of the hurt I felt for a love lost. The way I went about it was wrong but - at the time - I didn't think it was. I felt like I was doing the right thing for me but my judgement was severely clouded.

I never intended to commit a crime but I didn't tell them that. There was little point in saying it because they would never believe me. From their faces, they already didn't believe half of what I'd said to them.

'Anything else you'd like to add?' he asked.

I shook my head. There was nothing else to say. They'd seen the camper van, they'd pulled me over, they'd discovered the dead body. What else was there?

'There is one more thing I am curious about,' he said.

I waited for him to continue.

'When the body was found you said it was your wife... Why?'

'Because I had strong feelings for Emma. Your colleagues finding us shattered the illusion I'd created in which she was alive. By saying it was my wife - technically that would mean Emma would still be alive and well somewhere. I didn't want to think of her as deceased. I didn't want to know she was gone...'

With the exception of the whirring tape, the room fell silent once again.

'Are you sure there is nothing else you want to add?' the officer asked again, if only to break the silence.

I shook my head.

The only thing I was curious about now is what the actual charges would be that they'd raise against me. I was at a dead end, there was nothing else to know.

The officer leaned forward and turned the recorder off.

Author Bio

Matt Shaw is the author of over 200 published works. As well as appearing in a number of anthologies, Matt's work has been translated into French, German, Korean and Japanese. His work has also been adapted into graphic novels and - more recently - film.

Having successfully crowdfunded a feature film, in 2018 Matt Shaw adapted his best-selling novel MONSTER into a screenplay (with Shaun Hutson acting as script consultant) and then went on to direct it himself. The film starred Rod Glenn, Tracy Shaw (*Coronation Street*), Laura Ellen Wilson and Danielle Harold (*Eastenders*). Having broken his "film cherry", Matt is currently producing two more feature films - one an original piece which he wrote for screen (*Next Door*) and a second based on another of his novellas (*Love Life*).

Matt tours both the UK and the US on regular book signings but - if you're unable to get to where he is - there is also a store where you can purchase signed merchandise direct from him over on ETSY. Simply look up *The Twisted World of Matt Shaw* where you'll find exclusive downloads, his infamous *DeadTed* bears and more...

Want to stay up to date with Matt? He can be found on Twitter, Instagram and Facebook. There is also a fan club which has exclusive stories, early reads, behind the scenes information and a whole lot more - available on Patreon!

Printed in the USA
CPSIA information can be obtained
at www.ICGtesting.com
LVHW010321010224
770597LV00025B/678